GET SET! SWIM!

By Jeannine Atkins
Illustrated by Hector Viveros Lee

Lee & Low Books, Inc. · New York

To Emily Atkins Laird.
With thanks to Craig Collins
for his inspirational coaching—J.A.

For Kara, Mariah, Nicolas, and Francis—H.V.L.

Text copyright © 1998 by Jeannine Atkins
Illustrations copyright © 1998 by Hector Viveros Lee
All rights reserved. No part of the contents of this book may be
reproduced by any means without the written permission of the publisher.
LEE & LOW BOOKS, Inc., 95 Madison Avenue, New York, NY 10016

Printed in Hong Kong by South China Printing Co. (1988) Ltd.

Book Design by Tania Garcia
Book Production by The Kids at Our House

The text is set in 14 pt. Clearface
The illustrations are rendered in watercolor and pencil

10 9 8 7 6 5 4 3 2 1
First Edition

Library of Congress Cataloging-in-Publication Data
Atkins, Jeannine.
Get set! Swim!/by Jeannine Atkins;
illustrated by Hector Viveros Lee.—1st ed.
p.   cm.
Summary: A young Puerto Rican girl learns an important
lesson about pride and victory from her mother.
ISBN 1-880000-66-0
[1. Swimming—Fiction. 2. Puerto Ricans—United States—Fiction.]
I. Lee, Hector Viveros, ill. II. Title.
PZ7.A8634Ge 1998
[E]—dc21   97-31410
                    CIP AC

essenia's ponytail swished as she skipped downstairs. "Hurry, Mami," she called. This was Jessenia's first year on the swim team, her first meet at a rival team's pool. At the door Mami tucked a box into her purse and pinched her scarf together against the cold.

Jessenia raced her brother Luis down the street.
"Watch where you're going!" Mami said. "Stick together."

At the community center, Jessenia climbed on the bus and sat with Ana. When Luis tried to balance on the seat behind him, Mami settled him down by talking about when she'd been a girl in Puerto Rico. "Our house was so close to the ocean that it stood on stilts," Mami said. "We used to slide down grassy hills on palm leaves. The sky was very, very blue."

"Like that?" Luis pointed to the sky outside the window.

"No." Mami looked over the tall, crowded buildings. "This sky isn't blue enough."

Jessenia was tired of the dreamy way Mami spoke about the brilliant blue sky and sea that seemed to stretch forever. She pressed closer to the older girls in the seat ahead of her.

"Weston won by eight points last time," Nicole said. "We never win meets away from home."

"In Puerto Rico there are green lizards that cling to whatever they bite," Mami told Luis. "We girls used to hang them from our ears."

UNIFIED TRANSPORT

Luis put his thumbs to his earlobes and waggled his fingers like lizards. Jessenia turned to the window, thinking about how her mother had never learned to swim. Mami had made sure that she and Luis got swimming lessons. But it took more than dreams to win a race.

Jessenia was scared. How could they compete against the lucky girls who lived in these houses? As the space between the houses widened, so did the empty space inside Jessenia.

The bus stopped at Weston school. Mami kissed the top of Jessenia's head. She smiled as if she were breathing in a garden, though Jessenia knew her hair smelled just like the pool.

"Te amo," Mami said.

"I love you, too," Jessenia replied.

In the locker room, the girls pulled on their swimsuits and tucked their ponytails into caps. They stretched in the hallway as Coach Estes said, "Don't worry because the pool here is bigger. Everyone is equal in the water."

"Their pool probably isn't broken half the winter," Nicole muttered. "There are more girls on their team."

"Just keep your eyes on where you're going," Coach advised. "Now get in there and win!"

The first race was for the older swimmers. The water's surface broke with thundering dives. Jessenia cheered. It was hard to tell one girl from another until they turned. Then Jessenia recognized the way Nicole pulled in her knees before whipping them out. She sped ahead and rammed triumphantly into the wall.

Soon it was Jessenia's turn to stand on the edge of the pool between two girls from the other team. The overhead lights buzzed. The pool hummed. Jessenia rocked from toe to heel. She tried to breathe long and deep into her belly, the way Coach had taught her, but her short breaths caught at the back of her tongue.

Mami waved. Luis waggled his fingers like lizards. Jessenia's feet pressed flat on the smooth platform.

"Get ready," the coach called.

Goggles snapped as the girls pulled them on. Jessenia leaned toward the water. The empty space inside her seemed to fill with the marvelous blue that Mami remembered from Puerto Rico. The pool was exactly blue enough.

"Get set!"

"Go!"

The girls dived. The quiet, still water turned frothy and loud. Water streamed off Jessenia's goggles and rushed past her ears. She stretched her arms as long as Mami did when she talked about the great, wide sea. Then Jessenia caught sight of the girl in the next lane moving ahead. Jessenia gulped in some water. Her tired legs sank. She kicked hard again until one finger touched the end of the pool. She splashed up and gasped for air.

"Great race!" Coach Estes gave her a hand out. "You just lost a few seconds at the end when you looked to the side."

Mami was there and hugging her before Jessenia could warn her and Luis that they'd get wet.

"I'm so proud of you," Mami said.

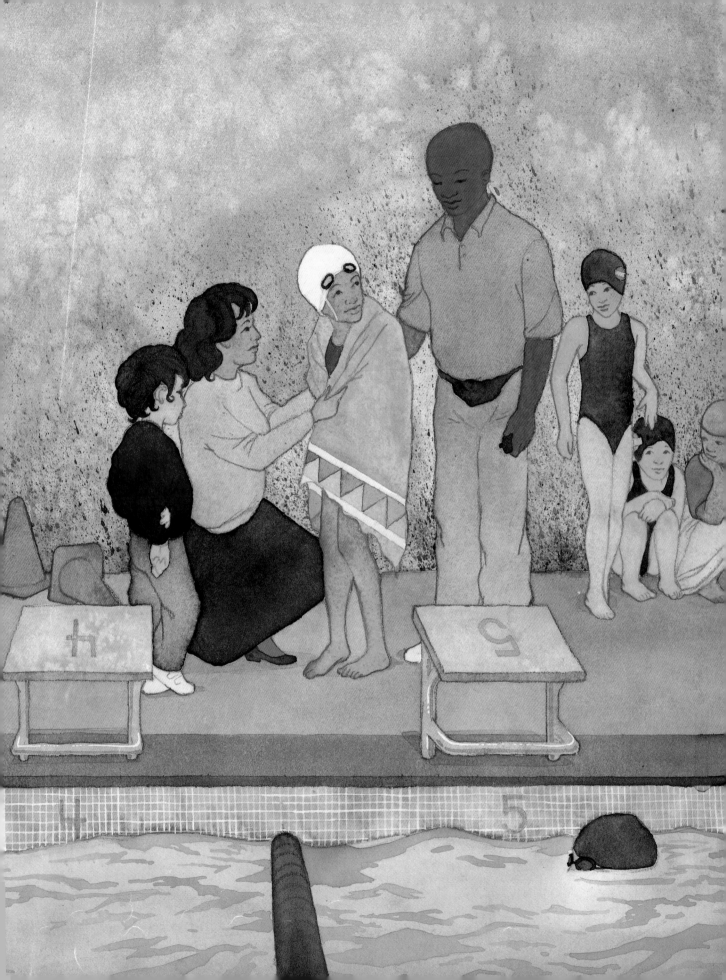

Jessenia pulled on a sweatshirt to watch more races. As the afternoon wore on and it became clear they were going to lose the meet, Jessenia cheered even louder and hugged her friends harder.

When it was her last turn to swim again, Jessenia tried to fill herself with calming air, but she kept taking quick, nervous breaths. She shifted her weight from one foot to the other. She wondered if she could swim fast enough to win.

Jessenia rose to her toes. She curled her arms and shoulders like a wave. *You can do it.* Jessenia seemed to hear her mother's voice as her hands broke the water.

She sped ahead, fast, faster, not only for herself and for her team, but for Mami, too. She didn't look back. She didn't look to the side. Jessenia swam with all the strength of her mother's dreams for her. Then her fingers tapped the wall.

Joyful girls pulled Jessenia from the pool, crying, "You won! You won!"
Jessenia turned to her mother and said, *"Te amo."*
"I love you, too," Mami smiled.

When the meet was over, the girls changed and dried their hair. Mami gave Jessenia a box as they stepped outdoors.

"*Gracias.*" Jessenia laughed as she pulled out earrings shaped like lizards. She slipped them on and danced a little salsa to make the earrings wiggle.

"Let's go, Jessenia!" Ana said.

The sky had turned a brighter blue. Their team would win another time, Jessenia knew. She spun around to call, "We'll be back!"